Introc

A Note to Parents, Teachers & Other Grown-Ups

"There are stories all around you just waiting to be told."

This is the message I've taken to thousands of aspiring writers and young readers during the past school year. And it is the message that has allowed both this series and the second installment of adventures to be told.

As a long-time magazine writer, I spent countless hours on my computer and phone; conducting interviews, doing research, pitching story ideas. It was only when I encountered a bit of downtime that I realized that my poodles were living a secret life; a life I had paid little attention to because of job demands; a life that was doggone funny. So, I did what any good wordsmith would do; I took out my pen and began to capture the adventures.

It took a few years of stop-and-go writing and editing, some children's writing classes and chats with teachers, librarians, book people and friends, but the perseverance and learning curve were well worth it. I can honestly say, I love what I do.

So, it is my belief that one need not travel far and wide to find a good tale. My tales happen in my home, almost on a daily basis. A petite, fussy redhead is added to the posse and Mrs. Flout and *The Frenchmen* must respond. The family takes a seaside vacation, encounters a slight change in plans, and needs to reset their inner compasses. It's all in a day's, week's or season's work living with furry friends. It's all entertaining. And what makes it work, is that through loveable little characters, it teaches us life lessons as we make our way in the world.

The observation of events and details all around us is not only critical for up-and-coming authors, but I believe, a valuable skill to acquire for a *bone-a-fide* good life—where we appreciate the daily fun and joy in the simplest of events.

Happy Tales,
Chrysa Smith

Posse: *A group of friends or associates*

Dedicated to Archie and Daisy,
The Humble and the Humbling

The Adventures of the Poodle Posse

by Chrysa Smith

Illustrated by Pat Achilles

THE WELL BRED BOOK

In the same series,

The Case of the Missing Steak Bone / Who Let the Dogs Out?

earlier adventures of the original posse

The Princess and the Frenchmen

"Oh, my," sang Mrs. Flout, as she walked into her living room, "And now there are three."

Of course, Mrs. Flout was talking about Daisy, the newest addition to her curly-haired poodle family. Daisy was the only girl and the newest poodle that had just come to live with the round, rosy-cheeked Francine Flout and her two little Frenchmen, Woody and Archie. A young redhead, little Daisy was bursting with energy. Nobody knew just what life would be like with three poodles, or that fussy little Daisy — the Princess, was about to turn Francine Flout's quiet home inside out and upside down.

Nice going, Woody thought, as he stared at Archie from the old, faded Persian rug. You see, Archie was the guy who took a long walk one night to rescue the little princess, and a strange mix of other homeless dogs. Since Daisy came, the little princess had taken over Mrs. Flout's comfy, green chair, which shifted Woody from his most favorite place down to the floor. Because Archie had a very soft spot in his heart for homeless dogs, Princess Daisy was now part of the Flout family, which meant a whole lot of changes taking place.

Now Mrs. Flout was both a first-class cook and an even better gardener. During the warm summer months, her garden was full of pretty, overflowing red and pink and purple flowers and rows of vegetables that stood up straight in the brilliant sun. In fact, her garden was so lovely, that she was chosen by the ladies of the town's garden committee to be on

the tour. And, the proud Mrs. Flout was spending extra time in the garden, with Daisy by her side or on
the lounge chair, and Woody and Archie lying in the
shade of the big Birch tree.

Both Archie and Woody got bumped out of all of their favorite places — in the living room, on the patio and in Mrs. Flout's bed. Before Princess Daisy came, Woody, the apricot-colored, first-born, would take his proper place next to Mrs. Flout, with his head on the pillow. Woody and Mrs. Flout would lie facing each other, both snoring and blowing warm breezes into each other's eyes. When Francine Flout let out a snore, Woody's ears would fly up in the air. When Woody let out a snore, Mrs. Flout's eyelashes would flutter. Of course, Archie would curl up like a little black ball of fur at the bottom of the bed, right next to Mrs. Flout's feet, keeping them warm and toasty all night long. But that was then.

Now, since Princess Daisy's arrival, she had chased Woody down from the pillow to Mrs. Flout's feet, which shifted poor Archie away from his mom

altogether; at the opposite corner of the bed. If either
Woody or Archie dared to come between her and
Mrs. Flout, Princess Daisy would curl up the left corner of her mouth, show her sharp little teeth and let
out a snarl. It was most unladylike, but as far as she
was concerned, Mrs. Flout was *her* new mom — *her*

very own person to love and be loved by. This was way too good to let anyone get in the way, even other members of the Flout family.

You must know that Daisy was a dreamer. She would lie around looking at Mrs. Flout's poodle books, which showed pictures of the famous French Female Poodles of Paris. They dressed in fancy clothes and lay on fluffy, plush, pink pillows. Now

that Mrs. Flout fell totally in love with the Little Princess, Daisy thought she might just be on the road to the life that she so deserves; the life of a princess.

But to Woody and Archie, Mrs. Flout was their mom too. And since Daisy came to live there, life was just not the same. Why, even Mrs. Flout did not seem the same. She bought Daisy a pink rhinestone

collar and matching leash, she spoke to Daisy with special words like honey and sweetie and princess. Woody and Archie even saw her knitting a little pink purse for Daisy to carry her bones in. But worst of all, she blamed Woody and Archie for anything broken, torn, misplaced or eaten. *This is an outrage!* thought Woody as he paced back and forth across the Persian carpet, *I must come up with a plan.*

Even sweet, quiet Archie was beginning to have thoughts of his own. *If I hadn't brought all of those dogs here, we wouldn't be having this problem. It would still be the two of us; Mrs. Flout's two, little Frenchmen.* But just as Archie was thinking about what he had done, Woody jumped up and headed for the kitchen. Daisy was in Mrs. Flout's arms, giving her a lick and a kiss goodbye, as Mrs. Flout was headed down the street to bring a bouquet of freshly picked flowers and a few juicy red tomatoes to her friend and neighbor, Mrs. Hemmings.

"All right my Princess, I have to put you down," Mrs. Flout laughed as she gave Daisy a big kiss on top of her curly red locks. "Come along, my little Frenchmen," she called to Woody and Archie, "It's such a beautiful day outside, you could all use a little fresh air."

As she led them out into the backyard, she gave them all a smile and a warning, "Now behave." And in an instant, Mrs. Flout was gone.

You don't have to tell us to be good, Woody

thought, as he eyed Daisy sprawled across the lounge chair. That used to be his spot as well until Daisy came. Archie found a nice, shady lump of grass and stretched out his paws. Woody came and joined him under the big birch tree.

As the two Frenchmen sat there feeling sorry for themselves, the loose flap in the fence came flying open. It was 'the guys' — the funny collection of four-pawed creatures that had all lived together back at the shelter. There was Topsy, the cute Terrier with

big hair and Freckles the Dalmation. For some rea-son every dog liked him. There was Potsy, the really pudgy Pug with big eyes and last but definitely not least, Big Benny — the Bulldog with the wide body, wrinkled face and a constant pool of drool that fell out of the side of his mouth.

Daisy looked over and yawned; so bored with ordinary dogs — dogs that clearly had no royal blood. Big Benny gave Woody a nudge with his nose, saying, "Hey, what's with the red head over there?"

Woody looked at Archie, Archie looked back and said, "Well, Mrs. Flout calls her Princess."

Benny laughed so hard that Topsy's hair began to shake. "Princess? Well maybe the Poodle Princess needs a crown. Come on, boys," Benny ordered his gang, "let's give the Princess what she deserves."

Now, Big Benny got his name not only because of his size, but because he was the boss. Topsy, Freckles and Potsy would go along with just about anything Benny could dream up. They all nodded in agreement, and followed Benny into Mrs. Flout's prize-winning flower patch. Right about now, Daisy perked up. She knew that something bad was going on and it might have to do with her. She just wasn't

sure what it was. Woody and Archie were a little nervous too. They didn't mind the gang putting Princess in her place, but upsetting Mrs. Flout's garden was clearly a bad idea. As much as Mrs. Flout loved the dogs and let them sit with her and sleep with her, Mrs. Flout's garden was the place where she drew the line. She knew her Frenchmen, and even the Little Princess would not know how to treat a prize garden.

First of all, if a butterfly happened to flutter by, you might find Archie kicking up rows of red roses, while chasing it out of the yard. Woody might just get the call to lift his back leg on a Rose Bush, or piddle on some pink Petunias. No, it was too risky for a gardener like Mrs. Flout to worry about. So she made some pretty strict rules for her garden.

Benny, Topsy and Freckles began plucking up Mrs. Flout's flowers; one-by-precious one. Woody and Archie tried to stop the gang, but they just went on their merry way, gathering the flowers and winding them into a circle for a crown.

"Hey, Little Princess," Benny called to Daisy, "Why don't you come over here and get your crown?"

Well, by this time, Topsy and Freckles and Potsy were in the act too, and maybe, just maybe, for the first time in her life, Daisy was a little bit scared.

"What's the matter," Benny called out in a girl-like voice, "Are you chicken? I thought you were a Poodle Princess!" All the gang howled with laughter, as Daisy shot off her chair and hid behind her two big brothers, Woody and Archie. She was shaking. Archie looked at Woody, Woody looked at Archie and yelled to Benny, "Hey, that's enough. Daisy may be a princess, but now, you have ripped up the garden of our mom. And our mom is the lady who helped you

17

find a good home. You are scaring a little girl who never did anything to you. So gather your drool, pull in your wrinkled jaw and behave like the best Bulldog I have known you to be. Clean up this mess."

Daisy and Archie shot Woody a look of great surprise. Woody was actually taking care of his little sister for the very first time. He stood up for what was right.

Benny's head hung low. He sucked up his drool, drew in his face and said in a very low voice to Woody, Archie and Daisy, "I'm sorry."

You see, Benny was really a good boy. But sometimes, his size and the fact that he spent so much time without a family meant that he could forget his canine manners.

"All right, boys," Benny ordered his gang, "Let's go to work and get this joint cleaned up."

The crew of dogs looked like a tornado, as they dove into the flower patch. They cleaned up the mess and very quietly, walked over to Daisy, who was still shaking.

"Here, these are for you," Benny said, as he presented Daisy with a bouquet of flowers from the garden.

Daisy's fear turned to surprise again, as she watched Benny, Topsy, Potsy and Freckles march back out of the yard, through the open flap. As usual, Woody and Archie looked at each other, then turned back to look at Daisy, but she was gone. *Uh, oh,* they thought, as they flew back into the house through the dog door.

They searched high and low. They looked in the kitchen and under the green chair. But just then, the door opened as Mrs. Flout came home from Mrs. Hemmings' house. In front of her was Daisy, with that bouquet of flowers in her mouth, ready to give to Mrs. Flout.

Woody and Archie were sure that Mrs. Flout would be furious to see the flowers in Daisy's mouth. She wasn't. She put down her purse, went over to Daisy and said, "Oh, I knew you were the most precious Little Princess I could ever find. Did you pick these just for me?"

At that moment, Woody and Archie stood there, tongues hanging out of their mouths. They couldn't believe what they were seeing.

"Well, would you look at that," Woody said to Archie, "She's not getting in trouble for picking flowers. She's getting praise." But as Woody was thinking the worst about Daisy again, she lifted her front paw and pointed to Woody and Archie.

"Oh, I see," said Mrs. Flout, "My whole family picked these for me. Well, how wonderful. You know you don't belong in the garden, but I am just so happy you three are getting along."

As she walked over to put the flowers in some water, Mrs. Flout was talking out loud to herself, "1 wasn't sure about adding a third poodle to the family. But now I see that I have such a way with poodles, I could add a few more. Right my little ones?"

No Dogs Allowed!

No Dogs Allowed! Mrs. Flout shouted.

Woody, Archie and Daisy froze in place as their mom put down the beach bag and chair she had brought along for the family vacation. She stared at a tall metal sign that read, *No biking. No roller skating. No loud music. No dogs.*

No Dogs? Woody, Archie and Daisy's ears shot up one by one, like six sharp arrows doing *the wave.* Could they have heard right? "Well, that's just great!" Woody snarled, "A fine beach vacation this will be." Daisy pointed to the lovely rhinestone crown on her head. She always wore it when she left the house, ever since she had read about the famous French Poodles of Paris. "No, no, no," Woody shot back, "It doesn't matter, even if you were a real princess. There are just some places where those of us with four paws and fur are just not welcome."

While Woody and Daisy were stuck in their problem, Archie had wandered over to the dunes and found a Yellow Lab out for a walk with his owner. They sniffed, wagged tails and before long, Archie made a friend. Along the way, he found out about a special place where the Yellow Lab and other dogs went to have their very own vacation. "It's called a dog park," Archie proudly told Woody. Woody lowered his dark brown eyes, glared at Archie and said, "Archie, do you know any park that's not a dog's park?"

"Oh, my," sang Mrs. Flout, "I wonder what dog families do at the shore?" A gentleman walking a Yellow Lab stopped by her side when he heard her talking. "Well, the dog park is very nice," he said as if she had asked him, "There's lots of room for dogs to run, a pool to cool off in, some toys to play with, and of course, lots of new friends to make."

Mrs. Flout was most grateful, and she gave a hearty thanks to the gentleman. "I am Francine Flout," she added, as she went to shake his hand. "Hi. I'm Mayor Sandpiper." Woody's ears shot up. *Well,* he thought, *Mayor Sandpiper is just the guy to take care of our little beach problem.* Woody pushed past everyone and stood right at the mayor's feet. His tail was wagging, eyes adoring, but just as the mayor bent down to give Woody a little pat on the head, Mrs. Flout rounded up the troops, "Come on, my little Princess and my Frenchmen. We're going to the dog park."

Woody stretched out his paws and lay across the road like a road block. He was acting like a little kid throwing a temper tantrum. He wouldn't budge. "Come on Woody, " Mrs. Flout told him, "You'll miss all the fun."

"Some fun that will be," Woody frowned, "Going to another park is not a real vacation."

Archie jumped in, "Maybe it will be more fun than our park. After all Woody, you've never been to this park before."

As the Flout family walked along, Daisy looked at her reflection in one of the store windows, "Oh, I wonder what I should wear?" she said.

Woody moaned. "For Pete's sake, a park is a park. There are always those people who run around and chase balls like us dogs. There are always a few of those little gray fellows with the bushy tails that collect nuts and race up and down the trees with them. I never know what they're doing. And then there are always a couple of good smelling bushes — you know — for when nature calls. That's about it."

"What a grump," Archie said to Daisy, "I don't care if he mopes around the entire week. I want to go to the dog park. I promised that Yellow Lab that I would be there."

Daisy agreed as she was trying on different crowns and collars, "I want to go too. You never know when a camera crew might be filming a movie and might just need a good-looking dog. Now which of these crowns do you think is best?"

"You guys go ahead and get your hopes up and your crowns on if you want," Woody warned, "You'll see. You'll be disappointed."

Mrs. Flout yelled, "Come on, my posse. This is a family vacation and the whole family is going to the dog park, including you, Woody."

She shot Woody a look that made him hide his eyes under his paws. He knew he was acting more like a little puppy than the oldest and top dog, but he had counted on romping in the sand, strolling through the surf, chasing the ocean waves and barking at the Horseshoe Crabs. Isn't that what a beach vacation is all about anyway? All that great stuff wouldn't happen now. That sort of fun doesn't happen at a park. It only happens at the beach.

Woody slowly stood up and slowly trailed behind Mrs. Flout, Archie and Daisy as they made their way to the dog park. It was a little walk to the park and the Flout family looked like a parade. Mrs. Flout was the leader. Behind her was Archie with his walking stick in his mouth. He thought he would take it to the dog park with him and share it with the Yellow Lab. Then Daisy followed with her rhinestone crown on top of her head, and her little pink knitted purse which she used to carry her bones. It was also a good place to stash any great treasure she might find. And last, but not least was Woody. This was so unlike Woody. As the top dog, Woody was always first. He was first to eat, first to sleep, first to be petted. But not on this day. This day was different.

33

"We're almost there, my little posse," Mrs. Flout cheerfully said with a smile, "Oh, I've heard about dog parks and how much fun they are," she added, "You guys are going to have so much fun!"

Right, Woody thought as he raised his eyes to see a big, dark chain link fence with gates and locks. This was not like any park any members of the posse had ever seen. Woody looked at Archie, who looked at Daisy, who looked back at Woody.

"Told you it would be disappointing," Woody said smartly.

"This looks like a place for dogs with no homes," Archie said with a shaky voice.

"I doubt anyone here could even appreciate my beautiful crown," added Daisy.

But Mrs. Flout just kept going, and before long, the posse was on the inside of the park, looking out. It did look a little like a cage, but just a lot bigger. The posse stood together, once again frozen in place. They didn't know what to make of the park, and Mrs. Flout's excitement. They all turned around together, slowly, like a chorus line. And one by one, their eyes grew big as they saw things they had never seen before.

First of all, there wasn't a stitch of grass — no bushes, no trees. The entire park was stone; lots and lots of stone. There was a big blue plastic pool filled with water. The posse thought it was a great big water bowl. But, just as one little Chihuahua went over to take a drink, a Great Dane did a cannonball into the pool. That meant the pool had to be refilled. There were strange structures and wooden tires that some dogs were playing on and a short water fountain, which had to be where they kept the clean water.

"Where on earth are we?" Woody asked.

At that moment Mayor Sandpiper came over with his Lab by his side. "Welcome to our dog park." he said.

The posse wasn't sure what to think, but the Yellow Lab came over and tugged at the end of Archie's walking stick. Before long, they were off running through the stones, jumping into the pool. Then, a beautiful white, Maltese came over to Daisy, lifted her paw and pointed to Daisy's pink purse. She twisted her rhinestone collar around and showed Daisy the purse her mom made her. It was just as beautiful. So before long, Daisy and the Maltese were off sharing royal stories, comparing collars, talking about crowns and purses.

And then there was Woody. Once again, this was so unlike him. Woody was left alone, left last, left to figure out what he was doing in this strange place. "Woody, " Mrs. Flout called, "Come here please." Mayor Sandpiper was standing with Mrs. Flout, with his hands behind his back. He reached around and pulled out a ball. He reached out again and pulled out a rope toy. Woody's eyes grew big as the Mayor began a game of fetch with Woody — his most favorite game. Before long, about seven other

dogs were playing too, behind the picnic table and in the big blue drinking pool. Mrs. Flout chatted with the Mayor, who introduced her to some of his town friends. She quickly learned that some dogs brought their owners to the dog park every day. While the dogs had fun with each other, their owners made new friends too.

After two hours of having fun playing in the park, Mrs. Flout gathered the troops to come together to return to their beach house. Again, they marched back to the house, one by one, like a parade. But this time, Mrs. Flout was first, Woody was right behind her, proudly carrying the ball Mayor Sandpiper had given to him. Then there was Archie, along with the Yellow Lab he had befriended. And then there was Daisy, with her stylish, new Maltese friend. They would all go back to the Flout's house for a **bone-b-que,** some TV and a good night's sleep. The new

friends would stay for a sleepover. After all, there was always lots of room at the Flout house for an extra furry friend.

As they got ready for bed, Mrs. Flout looked at the posse and their two new friends. She gave them each a place on the bed to put their paws up for the night. As the excitement of the day wore off, the Flout household was finally silent. Just as Mrs. Flout turned off the light, Woody whispered to Archie, "Well, maybe the dog park wasn't so bad after all. I guess, if I had to, I'd even go back tomorrow."

Now that you have read the adventures, track your favorite characters, stories and events from book 2—The *Princess and the Frenchmen/ No Dogs Allowed*!

Which adventure is your favorite and why?_____

_____

Who is your favorite character and why?_____

_____

What surprised you in these adventures?_____

_____

What makes you laugh?_____

_____

These adventures contain lessons about getting along and moving along. What lessons did you take away from these tales?_____

_____

Now that you know the characters in the series, what type of adventure would you create for them?_____

_____

_____

What type of adventure could you write, based on the people, pets and places in your life?_____

_____

_____

Want to get started writing? Share your ideas and comments? Get feedback for your stories? Find out if I'll be at your school or local bookstore?

Log onto my website: www.wellbredbook.net, drop me a line by email to chrysasmith@verizon.net or by regular mail to The Well Bred Book, PO Box 50, Pt. Pleasant, PA 18950.

I love to hear from *posse* fans and I always write back. Please be sure to include your name and address so I can respond.

Happy Tales to You!

Earlier adventures can be found in book 1: ***The Case of the Missing Steak Bone/Who Let the Dogs Out?***

'Work can wait another 30 minutes.
There are more important things to do--
like throwing sticks'
-- and giving thanks

For partnership in book design, production and promotion—
Pat Achilles

For reviews, research, informed suggestion and
general helpfulness—
Denise Bash, MaryFran Bontempo, Leslie Clark,
Carmen Ferreiro-Esteban, Linda Hastie, Diane Smith,
Mary Smith, the staff and students at Conshohocken
Elementary, the staff and students at Asa Packer Elementary

For general inspiration—
Mark , Dane , Dottie, Bob, Woody, Archie, Daisy, Bobby,
Geezie, Linda, Nan, Pat, Karen, Perry, Jay, Ruth, Cleta,
Stacy, Rowena & all of the teachers, librarians, parents,
young readers & friends who have helped make
this series a reality

First time meeting the posse?

Author Chrysa Smith is a recipient of the prestigious Mom's Choice Award for *The Adventures of the Poodle Posse (The Case of the Missing Steak Bone/Who Let the Dogs Out?)*—the first book in the series. The Mom's Choice Awards honors excellence in family-friendly media, products and services. An esteemed panel of judges includes education, media and other experts as well as parents, children, librarians, performing artists, producers, medical and business professionals, authors, scientists and others. Panel members include: Dr. Twila C. Liggett, ten-time Emmy-winner, professor and founder of Reading Rainbow; Julie Aigner-Clark, Creator of Baby Einstein and The Safe Side Project; Jodee Blanco, New York Times Best-Selling Author; LeAnn Thieman, Motivational Speaker and coauthor of seven Chicken Soup For the Soul books; and Tara Paterson, Certified Parent Coach and founder of the Mom's Choice Awards.

What have reviewers said?

Little curly haired poodles and their zany antics make for a fun read in *The Adventures of the Poodle Posse*. Author, Chrysa Smith shares her real life stories with her beloved poodles in this early-reader. Illustrator, Pat Achilles, highlights Smith's stories with adorable and friendly black and white illustrations. This fun and sometimes very silly book will engage young readers with pet-friendly stories that are a delight to read. Audiences will enjoy the light-hearted humor as they learn about sharing and caring. Readers will also have fun at the end of the book where they are encouraged to talk about the stories, characters and what makes them laugh the most. For a wonderful book that will encourage young readers to develop a love for pets and their silly antics, *The Adventures of the Poodle Posse* is a great read.

—Reviewer's Bookwatch, *The Midwest Book Review*

Find out more at **www.wellbredbook.net**

*Written, designed and printed
in the Greater Philadelphia Area.*